Haleh Rafi is a lifelong storyteller, educator, researcher, and pianist. Her love of literature and spirituality and her experiences in education, from early childhood through higher education, has led to several published book chapters and journal articles. Her storytelling approach to life has inspired a published collection of short stories titled *Epiphanies,* where she explored intuitive grasps of reality in everyday experiences.

Haleh Rafi grew up in Iran and went on a journey of immigration to different countries before finally landing in Melbourne, Australia. She is still a teacher and researcher who is captivating her audience with her storytelling voice or drawing their attention with the expressive sound of her piano.

To my father, who gave me my love of literature. May his soul rest in peace, and his memory never fade.

And to those striving for freedom and justice.

Haleh Rafi

THE FATHER

AUSTIN MACAULEY PUBLISHERS™

LONDON • CAMBRIDGE • NEW YORK • SHARJAH

A CIP catalogue record for this title is available from the British Library.

ISBN 9781035839261 (Paperback)
ISBN 9781035839278 (ePub e-book)

www.austinmacauley.co.uk

First Published 2024
Austin Macauley Publishers Ltd®
1 Canada Square
Canary Wharf
London
E14 5AA

I would like to express my gratitude to all those who shared details of their experiences during the demonstrations and arrests of the 2009 protests in Iran. Some of their words, expressions and sentences have been directly used within the story. I am also extremely grateful to Anita Rafi, my young and highly competent niece, and Mariam Elneta Nouri, my resourceful cousin, who agreed to review and edit my story. They are certainly the best editors a writer could wish for.

Preface

Chinua Achebe, the great Nigerian novelist, poet, and critic, chooses to write in African English to express "a new voice coming out of Africa, speaking of African experience in a world-wide language." When he is asked, in an interview, if an African can ever learn English well enough to be able to use it effectively in creative writing, his answer is, "Certainly yes!" But when the interviewer asks him if the African can ever learn to use English like a native speaker, Achebe responds, "I hope not!" Achebe elaborates his comment as below,

"The African writer should aim to use English in a way that brings out his message best without altering the language to the extent that its value as a medium of international exchange will be lost. He should aim at fashioning out an English which is at once universal and able to carry his peculiar experience."

I cannot use English like a native speaker. However, inspired by Achebe, I dared to write my novel in English to express my voice in a world-wide language, hoping that it would carry my 'peculiar experience' across the world. As one of my readers commented on my previous book, the way I use English in my stories is 'my signature'.

Haleh Rafi

One

"I disliked the advertisement because ..."

The distant clicking sound of ice cubes being dropped into a glass distracted Ava. "How could it be? When did he come home? Was he already at home when we came in?" she pondered with fright.

Ava was in her bedroom with her English teacher. Although the bedroom was at the end of a long hall far from the kitchen, the cacophony of tumbling ice cubes still seemed tumultuous. To Ava, it was an intimidating sound, a sign of a bad omen.

Ava was in the middle of her response to an IELTS speaking question, describing an advertisement she disliked. She had already explained the introductory parts: what the advertisement had been about, and where and when she had first seen it. Now she needed to articulate what she had disliked about it. But the distracting sound from the kitchen made her forget what she had previously planned to say. Listlessly, she looked at the cue card in her hand and tried to focus.

"I disliked the advertisement because ..."

The father usually went to work late in the morning and stayed at work until late in the evening. Whenever Ava had to have friends over, she arranged for them to come for short visits early in the afternoon when she was certain the father was not at home. Now she was taken aback by his presence. *"Maybe he will go back to his study if I wait long enough. Then the teacher can leave without having to meet him."*

Ava did not know what to do. She did not want the father to hear them talking. Impulsively she stood up, walked towards the bedroom door, and closed it. It was a sweltering hot day, and the bedroom did not have air conditioning. Closing the door would stop the feeble current that was coming in from the air conditioning in the living room. It meant they would soon become stifled. Ava took a deep breath, sat down at her desk, and continued her sentence in a quiet but angry tone.

"I disliked it because the advertisement took social justice movements for an opportunity to sell drinks … because it was disrespectful to all those people who had sacrificed for the sake of social change."

"Good!" said the English teacher. She could detect Ava's frustration, so she also spoke quietly. "Your anger is adding to its appeal!" she added with a smile. Ava smiled back, but her smile soon vanished when she began to bite her lower lip. The English teacher knew better than to ask any questions at such moments, so she continued with the related discussion topics.

"Are there plenty of advertisements in your country?"

"Why do you think there are so many advertisements coming out nowadays?"

"What are the different places where we often see advertisements?"

"Do advertisements influence your decision or choice of product?"

They studied for another ten minutes, but Ava was completely distracted. She could hear her father moving around the house, turning the television on and opening windows. Drops of sweat appeared on her forehead, and she could feel the perspiration trickling down her neck, "*Soon the back of my t-shirt will be wet.*"

"Can we have a shorter class today, please?"

Seeing her discomfort, the English teacher did not even ask for a reason, "Of course! Let us sum up, then."

The teacher opened her notebook, and they looked at some other speaking topics: What is a good book that you have read? What is a bad book that you have read? A good movie that you have watched, a bad movie that you have watched, a party you liked, a party you disliked, a character you admired, a character you despised, a dream that has come true, a dream that has not, music, sport, weather, food, transport, clothes, hobbies, neighbourhoods. To all these questions, Ava had prepared answers. Most of her answers were related to social justice. This way, she would be able to use the vast number of words and expressions she knew well and navigate over the topics impressively. As social justice was her main concern in life, not only did she know the jargon well, but the passion and enthusiasm were also reflected in her answers and made them more sophisticated.

The exam was in two months, but the English teacher knew that they had already covered all the necessary parts. She raised her head up from the notebook.

"Complete your notes on the last three topics we discussed today. That would be all. I think you are ready for the exam!"

Ava nodded and stood up. She slowly opened the door, glanced outside, and listened carefully while the teacher was packing. The apartment was hushed. *"Please God, let him be back in his study,"* she prayed.

They walked together through the hall towards the apartment door. In the living room, Ava saw the father standing next to the window, looking out. He had a glass of vodka in his hand. Hearing them coming into the room, he turned back. Ava's heart started to race. The English teacher, though, remained calm and politely greeted him. Looking at the girls with narrowed eyes, the father remained silent for five seconds and then he growled in his deep voice, "Who is this motherfucker?"

Ava was mortified. She quickly held the English teacher's hand and pulled her towards the door, snatched her manteau and scarf from the hook on the way, jumped out, and slammed the door behind her.

Two

15

Living with a tippler was not easy. It was not just the drinking, but, in Ava's words, "all the other crap that went with it." The father was the most formidable man on the planet, or so Ava thought. He was arrogant, with a foul mouth and an even fouler disposition, and his disagreeable behaviour was magnified every time he drank, which was every evening. He was verbally abusive. Profanity was his second language, and expletives were his jargon. He often raised his voice and spoke coarsely to people, and his words did hurt. He snapped at children when he did not like what they were doing and immediately told their parents that "the kid is bloody spoiled," even when he did not know the child or their parents at all. No matter what he was conversing about – commenting on a player's style in a soccer match, an employee working in a company, or a doctor who treated him recently – he cussed and cursed and swore. When interacting with people, he frequently used the most insulting language to intentionally offend them. Evidently, he was an outcast in society. People had gradually distanced themselves from him, and his world had become smaller and smaller until he was left in his one-man land.

Ava's mother was not of much help. She was a timid, quieted woman, a beauty who had withered like an exotic flower planted in an unfamiliar condition. She had flaming red hair and creamy skin, but an opaque film of deep grief shadowed her hazel eyes. For years, the father had abused her with constant hurtful criticism and berating. He highlighted her weaknesses, trivialised her action, and disparaged all her actions and even her own being. He made sure that all her friends were affronted. The father's bitter tongue had made her a solitary woman with no friend or family member around. All her friends were long scattered away as they did not want anything to do with her abominable husband. Being lonely for a long time had caused her to have to put up with persistent depressive disorder. She had low appetite, low energy, low motivation, and low self-esteem. She was dealing with general discontent and indecisiveness, and suffered from poor concentration and sleep deprivation. She was chronically tired and showed no interest or pleasure in any activities. Dysthymia had been embedded into her life and outlook.

Ava had inherited her mother's beauty: the creamy skin, the wide eyes, the full cheeks, the refined nose, and the lush wavy hair. But she did not have anything else in common with her. She loved her mother, but at the same time felt distanced from her. They simply did not understand each other's worlds. It had been years since they had talked about anything serious. Sometimes Ava brought her mother's attention to a topic she had read about in a book or something that she had discussed with a friend. Her mother tried to show some enthusiasm, but Ava could detect the indifference in her voice. Sometimes her mother ran into Ava in the kitchen and asked her about her friends or her studies. But Ava, again, could see that the questions were but formalities. She answered politely and superficially, but never related details. And, as if in a secret agreement, they never discussed the father and his negative influence on their lives.

Ava did not pity her mother. To Ava, she seemed self-content in her sequestered world. She had sensibly distanced herself from the father and occupied herself with life's routines and cycles. She cooked and cleaned and went grocery shopping. She had created a coping mechanism and delusion of reality that allowed her to dismiss the unfairness that she could not let go of. She sometimes wrote poems and read them aloud to herself. When Ava was a young child, her mother had told her a real story of how she used to live with her imaginary friends, talking to them, playing with them, even studying with them. Ava liked to believe that her mother was still living contentedly with her imaginary friends, interacting with them, and reading her poems to them. Therefore, she tried to leave her alone and not disturb her much.

Ava did not have any brothers or sisters. She and her parents resembled three separated islands in a vast ocean. They did not go anywhere together. They did not eat or watch movies together. Most of the time, they did not even talk to one another, and the apartment was almost always a silent, secluded place. The three of them were readers. Many hours during the day and the night, they silently conversed with books. Ava tried to avoid seeing her parents as much as she could and spent many hours out of the house. But when she was home with them, one could find Ava in her bedroom, her mother in her rocking chair in the living room, and her father in his study, reading.

Ava studied architecture. She had a brilliant mind and enjoyed calculating, designing, drawing, and building models. She loved studying architecture because she could set her mind in order by putting pencils on paper, cutting, shaping, and gluing. Having recently graduated, Ava was planning to continue her studies abroad. That was a plan to escape as well – the farther, the better. With distinction university grades, a few published articles in ISA journals, and good recommendation letters from her professors, she had a high chance of receiving a scholarship from the university she had in mind. Ava had applied for the university and only needed good grades in IELTS to complete her application. In only a few months, she would leave her country, her house, and the father forever.

While waiting and preparing for the IELTS exam, Ava also busied herself with the upcoming presidential election in the country. That year, many people, who were looking forward to a change in the system of governing in Iran, were supporting a certain candidate who – they believed – could improve the oppressive ruling system. Ava was fully engaged with the pre-election events and actively supported that candidate's campaign. Next to her interests in mathematics and art, she had a deep concern for social justice and aspired towards freedom. With a sublime heart, her life purpose was to right all wrongs, make strong the weak, and mend the broken.

At the time, Ava was also a spirited campaigner for women's right to higher education, self-determination, and liberation. She helped a group of activists who informed people about the injustices that happened in the country and called for action to change things. She truly travelled to remote villages to educate women! She taught the illiterate how to read and write and tried to help them become financially independent by finding ways to sell their handicrafts. She also talked to them to help them understand their human rights. Such activities were against the government's will and could have perilous consequences. But Ava was a single-minded girl, even if she saw herself as a 'multi-thoughted' one. She felt invincible, and despite the potential danger, she persisted in her acts of bravery without hesitation. The presidential campaign was now added to her daily activities, and Ava, along with some of her close friends, spent hours every day advertising, informing, and encouraging people to vote for their candidate.

Supporting presidential campaigns was an extremely controversial issue in those days. Some people did not trust the candidates who originally belonged to the body of the government. They argued that the candidates were taking advantage of the naïve youth to reach power and believed that the totalitarian government would not allow any change in the system, no matter which candidate was chosen. The father was among those who mistrusted them all. When he found out that Ava was working for the campaign, a war of words began in their house. For once, after a long time of silence, the apartment witnessed some interactions that, in fact, were more distancing than connecting. Ava and the father argued almost every night. The father started with scorning all of Ava's activities while shouting foul-mouthed obscenities. Once, in a fit of rage, he smashed his glass of vodka on the floor. Ava was silent for most of the time while he was shouting and made herself busy with anything at hand. She hoped the frenzy would pass. When she eventually responded, her answers were coldly uttered few-word sentences. Ava's nonchalant tone made the father even angrier, and he shouted even louder only to add to the downward spiral of their relationship.

Three

Ava was warming up her food in the microwave oven in the kitchen. She had her headphones on and was listening to Gloria Gaynor's "I Am What I Am" on her iPod, humming along. It was a warm, golden evening, and she was cheerful for no particular reason. The song, which started melodious and mellow, soon took up a jaunty beat. Ava was taking some dancing steps in front of the fridge when a dark shadow plummeted towards her. She looked up. It was the father, unshaved and ugly. Anticipating another useless argument, Ava turned up the volume of the music to avoid hearing what he had to say. She took her food from the microwave and tried to go out, but the father was standing right at the door, blocking her way. The father habitually swore at the government and all those who had fallen victim to its plans, including Ava and her friends. For a minute, Ava remained apprehensive, tight-lipped, and very tense. The father yelled, and the swear words that mixed with the songs' lyrics created an absurd situation. Suddenly, perhaps under the effect of the music, Ava decided that she had had enough. She firmly walked towards the kitchen door and pushed the father aside. She passed through, speaking in a commanding voice.

"Get out of my way, you coward! You cannot intimidate me. It is good that every day I see some brave people out there, or else I would think everybody in the world is as craven as you are!"

The father did not expect that. It was the first time Ava was reacting aggressively, confronting him and answering back. He stood open-mouthed, "Since when did she dare to …?" It seemed that their antagonism had moved to the next level – a more detrimental level. The shock of seeing Ava talking with such language had struck the father dumb, but he soon managed to bark back.

"What crap are you talking about? You dumb little twit! Your so-called votes don't count. You're no more than fucking puppets to promoting the government propaganda. And you will never win. The son of the bitch they have already chosen, no matter what you do."

To the father's surprise, Ava turned back and met his gaze.

"That's fine with me. Even if I'm doomed to lose the game, I will make it a pyrrhic victory for them. They will always remember what we wanted and what we did."

She began to move towards her bedroom to show that that was the end of the conversation. At her bedroom door, though, she quietly mumbled a few words.

"I take a leap of faith every day."

The father was following her, feeling the rage expand inside him.

"What did you blabber?!"

He was determined to continue the fight, showing her his contempt. But Ava went into her bedroom, slammed the door in his face, and locked the door. The father was frantic now. He shook the knob and hit the door hard with his fist.

"Open the fucking door!"

The loud knock gave Ava a shock, and she gasped back in fright. She stared at the shaking door, thinking that it might break if the father continued banging on it. But the father just went away, still yelling curse words. Ava sat on her bed, covered her ears with her hands, and rocking herself back and forth repeated her mantra of "*Why don't you just die? Why don't you just die? Why don't you just die? ...*"

Four

Ava hated her dipsomaniac father. That was what she constantly told herself. The father was poisonous and contaminated every place with his presence. There was an aura of menace about him that frightened everyone, and he was Ava's main source of embarrassment. On very rare occasions that Ava had company at home, her mind was continually occupied with worries and concerns, *"He might come into the room and begin to talk!"* She had to constantly find ways to prevent her friends from meeting the father; otherwise, she would be involved in the cringeworthy act of explaining and apologising for what he had said. Sometimes, she hated him so badly that she wished him dead, *"Why doesn't he just die? Things would be much easier that way."*

Ava's safety valve, what prevented her from going round the bend, was opposing the father in every possible situation. In fact, her presence and involvement in presidential campaigns were highly related to her opposition to the father. She enjoyed engaging in activities that he disapproved of. The more the father condemned something, the greater her enthusiasm to get involved with it. While commuting to the campaign, she had long self-conversations in her mind, trying to convince herself that what she was doing was the right thing to do, "*It is easy to limit your actions to complaining, to sit down and curse. It is easy not to do anything. Change needs effort ... and it certainly needs risk.*"

To fully oppose the father, Ava registered as a fixed member and attended the campaign almost every day from early in the morning until late at night. During those days, the campaign sites were full of young women fluttering about like a flock of excited butterflies, and Ava volunteered for almost every possible task at hand: planning question & answer meetings with people and encouraging them to vote; designing posters and holding them while standing silently in the streets to have passers-by read the messages; getting on random buses and traveling all the way to the terminal station just to talk to passengers and distribute flyers, and then taking another bus to return to the campaign. Ava was filled with excitement and enthusiasm and did so love those days. The resolute fight against evil enriched her life, "*I take a leap of faith every day just by walking through that door in the morning. I take a leap of faith by believing that it will be worth it, that it will all ultimately mean something.*"

In another world, Ava would be a perfect social activist. She knew life and understood people. She was a great conversationalist who talked to all sorts of people and thus was familiar with a wide range of ideologies. Outside her home, Ava was a talker, a chewer of ears. She continuously talked, made jokes, consoled, impressed, and inspired. Sometimes she found herself chattering only for the sheer delight of tossing out words into the bright air, as children enjoy sending up kites. One could not find her silent for a minute. She was proud of her talking habit and justified it by saying that talking was a reformer's trait. She was also a disciplined girl who did everything accurately and expected everyone else to be as conscientious as herself. This attribute of hers sometimes annoyed her friends, but she persisted as she thought diligence was a necessary aspect of a strong personality. Had she lived in a democratic country, Ava would make a difference to the lives of thousands of people. However, then and there, not only were her actions taken for granted, but she was unconsciously moving towards a dark abyss she was unaware of.

On the last day before the deadline of the election campaigns, Ava and her friends stayed out until very late at night. They were talking to people, convincing them to vote, and dropping flyers in the mailboxes. It was past midnight when they decided to call it a day and drove back home. In the car, they excitedly talked about their experiences with the twenty-kilometre-long chain that had been formed by literally hundreds of thousands of their candidate's supporters in one of the most important streets of the city. They had called the chain the 'Green Line', since green served as the official colour of their campaign. The waning gibbous moon shone brightly in the night sky and a cool pleasant breeze was blowing. In the empty streets, where there were no cars except theirs, Ava stuck her hand out of the car window. The green ribbon tied to her index finger danced in the wind. Green leaflets and banners could be seen everywhere. She was excited, and the anticipation of 'change for better' created glittering sparks in her eyes. She felt proud to have participated in a movement that would improve the lives of millions of people … or so it seemed to her. She truly believed that their tireless efforts deserved the reward of victory and would be well worth their while.

Ava and her friends went to their homes with deep hope in their hearts. What they were doing in those days was inspiring to many people. Their aspiration towards justice made even the most cynical people wonder if the change could really happen. After many dark years, hope had risen again in the country. Hope does strange things to people. It can make a tough situation more bearable. Human beings keep holding on to their hopes, even when their brains consider things impossible.

Five

Ava was lying down on her back in bed with her hands under her head, humming Peggy Lee's song "It's a Good Day" to herself. Her eyes were closed, and she was imagining herself lying on her back on the surface of water. The position was soothing, comforting, and appeasing. She had woken up on the first flush of the morning and was too excited to go back to sleep. The room was deep dark when she first opened her eyes, and Ava enjoyed observing the changes of different shades of colours through the blue curtains as the light cautiously found its way to her bedroom.

Ava loved her bedroom. She had painted the walls and decorated it herself. Sometimes she stood in the middle of the room, moved in a circle, and watched all the details. The bed, the dresser, the bookshelf, the desk, the wardrobe, the framed pictures, the wall calendar, the posters, and the chest of drawers were all situated beautifully and designed with colour harmony. The blue and brown tone hue granted a fantastic accent and a charming appeal to the place. From where Ava was lying, she could clearly see the wall calendar on which Friday the 12th was circled and highlighted in green, "*Oh, what a day it was!*"

The day before, Ava and her friends had voted early in the morning but stayed out till late in the afternoon roaming the streets and going from one voting centre to another. They were busy all day talking to people in the long queues outside the centres. There were so many who were supporters of the candidate Ava and her friends had campaigned for. Many people were first-time voters not because they were teenagers who had not been eligible to vote before, but because they had never had the interest or motivation to participate in the governmental elections.

It was a cool day for the middle of June. In one place, Ava and her friends had seen a large group of young men and women who had been listening to loud music from a stereo on the sidewalk. On any other day, they could have been arrested for the crime of disturbing the public morality. But that day, as hundreds of foreign journalists walked the city, covering the election, the government was letting them be, as the regime needed to show the world its capacity for tolerance. Ava could breathe hope in the air and remained in jovial mood long after she came back home. In the evening, to everyone's surprise, it suddenly started to rain. Everything was different. Everything would be different.

Ava opened her eyes, and the first thing she saw was the wall calendar again. It was Saturday the 13th. She never liked the number 13, but that day was different. It was supposed to be Victory Day! *This is the day that superstitions will also be broken down!*" Parts of the election results would have already been announced, but Ava could not turn on the television, which was in the living room. The father was at home, and Ava was not in the mood to fight with him. She did not want her day to be ruined by his rants. She waited until it was 8 o'clock, then she rose from bed, reached for the phone on the bedside table, and dialled her friend's number. She had told her friend that she would call her at 8. She did not want to call her too early in case her friend's parents were still asleep.

"Hello?"

Instead of the usual greeting, Ava started to sing the rest of the song she was singing to herself in a soft voice. She expected a scream of joy, a laugh or a funny banter. She expected her friend to update her with the latest statistics from different cities. But her friend was silent.

"Hello? Are you OK? What is it?"

Her friend was speaking with a soft sad voice.

"We lost!"

Ava could not believe this. Surely it was a prank. She laughed.

"OK! I am too excited for jests. Please give me the numbers."

Ava continued talking with plans for celebrations, where they should go, and who they should meet. Eventually, the extended silence on the other side of the phone worried her. She had to pause.

"Hello? Are you there?"

Ava heard a muffled sound through the phone. She listened carefully. It was her friend, sobbing. Ava's throat tightened. She tried to calculate the probability by reviewing the number of people they saw in the queues the day before. That did not make sense.

"But how? It can't be!"

Tears stung Ava's eyes, building up and rolling over her cheeks with the heat of a dying star. She sank to her knees next to her bed and raked strands of black hair from her forehead. The number 13 on the hanging wall calendar seemed to mock her. Blurry images of yesterday's events still marched in her mind: the smiles, the encouraging gestures, the happy words, the dancing green ribbons on the wrists, and the hope in the eyes of all those people in the voting queues.

"It just can't be!"

Six

Hope was all people had at the time. They hoped that the more liberal president would make their lives slightly better. The country was a dictatorship where any voice of criticism was brutally suppressed. According to the Constitution, the Supreme Leader made the final decision about all affairs of the State. People were aware that the president, as the head of the executive branch, had limited power and was only in charge of day to day running of the country. They knew that he could not make any changes to the government's structural policies. However, they believed that a strong president who had the support of the public could bring a certain level of freedom for them. Their expectations targeted the minimum human rights that so many people enjoyed in the world without knowing how privileged they were. They merely hoped for less government interference in their personal lives and adjustments to some rules like censorship of the printed media, the harassment by the morality police, the mandatory headscarves, and restrictions on different art forms.

The country was a dictatorship where any voice of criticism was brutally suppressed. According to the Constitution, the Supreme Leader made the final decision about all affairs of the State. People were aware that the president, as the head of the executive branch, had limited power and was only in charge of day to day running of the country. They knew that he could not make any changes to the government's structural policies. However, they believed that a strong president who had the support of the public could bring a certain level of freedom for them. Their expectations targeted the minimum human rights that so many people enjoyed in the world without knowing how privileged they were. They merely hoped for less government interference in their personal lives and adjustments to some rules like censorship of the printed media, the harassment by the morality police, the mandatory headscarves, and restrictions on different art forms.

. They hoped for some freedom of speech, just as much that they were able to openly criticise corruption and organised crime without being falsely accused of being an enemy to the country. In a country where people could be arrested for walking in the streets without a headscarf, for dancing, or for singing a song with critical content, even a bit of freedom would alleviate life.

Nevertheless, all the hope in people's hearts soon diminished when the election results came out. The more liberal candidate, for whom Ava and her campaign friends and many other people voted, did not win the election. As the father had anticipated, the candidate whom the dictatorship had already chosen was 'elected'. There were talks about electoral fraud and vote rigging. People said that the officials deliberately changed the result of the election by increasing the vote share of their favoured candidate. There were witnesses who reported missing ballot boxes and disappeared ballot slips in some places. They said that the contents of the boxes were checked, and the unfavourable slips were destroyed. People had to dismiss all their hopes for social reforms.

In the aftermath of the election, shocked people began to think about the best reaction they could have. Protesting was not legal in the country, and people did not think of it as an option. But frustration made people wonder if they could try. People came out of their houses, initially with no specific purpose. They gathered silently and walked aimlessly in the streets with heavy hearts. The situation had induced feelings of outrage within people as they thought their votes were stolen their rights to have a fair election were infringed upon.

Gradually, the small gatherings joined together and formed sporadic demonstrations. The fury and frustration in people's hearts soon turned into fuel that motivated them to raise their voices and ask for the annulment of the fraudulent election. They wanted the government to either recount the votes or hold another election. People were seen in the streets carrying placards that read, "Where is my vote?" Demonstrations, presently, became bigger. Young men and women took things a step further, and then older people cautiously joined the anti-government protests in different cities. One day there were tens of thousands of people in the streets, the next there were hundreds of thousands. Several massive protests were held around the country. Many protesters had green wristbands around their forearms or green scarves around their necks. Thus, the green colour of the campaign tied the people in unity and birthed 'The Green Movement'. Protests had no formal organisation. No one arranged the structure of the protests or the slogans that challenged the country's authoritarian clerical rulers.

Protesters braved the false twist in the election voluntarily, and slogans developed as events unfolded. There seemed to be new hope for people who were particularly delighted by the improvised nature of the protests.

The demonstrations were peaceful. People merely wanted the election to be repeated and expected that the government officials would listen to them and react justly. However, they were soon disappointed as the government was not responsive. To their dismay, several of the high-ranking government officials began congratulating the soon-to-be new, what people called 'president-[S]elect'. People were exasperated. In a few days, protests widened, and the gatherings became bigger; and one day, it was reported that more than two thousand people gathered in an iconic place in the capital city. Besides, a spontaneous plan went on where, every night at a certain time, people shouted their objections through their windows. Their uproar shook almost all the streets in various cities with a feeling of stupendous wholeness.

Subsequently, the government, that had underestimated people's resolve to fight for their rights, prohibited any forms of gathering, and the state officials announced that any unofficial demonstration would be illegal and not be tolerated. That was no empty threat. Feverish days and frantic nights began when the government police intervened.

Seven

"Remember what I told you about your voice?"

A young man with a brown cap stood next to Ava and was talking loudly to his friends. But by the way he moved his head around and looked at others, Ava could tell that he intended that other people around him could hear him as well.

"Your voice is your biggest weapon. Use it! Ask where your vote is!"

Ava's heart was beating fast. A few people began to shout and soon many more joined them. Ava's friend was very excited and screamed at the top of her lungs. The all-in-black riot police guards were standing at the other end of the street with five or six police trucks behind them. They were probably waiting for a signal because soon after people began to shout, several tear gas grenades were fired. Ava watched with horror as the grenades sailed into the air and landed in the middle of the street. Smoke was whizzing out the end of them. They would combust any second. The young man with the brown cap ran towards one of the tear gas canisters and kicked it back to the police. Ava gasped as it exploded in the air and consumed the guards in a cloud of tear gas. One of the tear gas canisters exploded right where Ava and her friend were standing and it did not take long for them to feel its suffocating power. The gas caused a severe burning sensation in their eyes. Ava's nose and throat burned as if she swallowed fire. Her eyes felt like flames licked them.

"Oh shit!"

Billowing clouds of tear gas hit the crowd and forced them to clear the square. Then the guards stampeded over and the crowd ran for their lives. Ava could hear loud bursts of bullets as well. Disoriented from the fog of explosions, people were running in different directions to save their lives. The guards cornered a group of men and women and started to beat them viciously with their clubs and kicked them with their military boots. Ava gripped her friend's hand tight in order not to lose her in the melee. The explosions kept going off and thick white smoke engulfed them. Ava pulled her friend's sleeve and motioned her to run. Her nose and mouth were stinging. She could barely see or breathe, but her friend's situation was much more grievous. She seemed to be in agony and running did not help in any manner. Despite the pain and difficulty in breathing, they both forced themselves to run till they reached a less crowded area. There, Ava's friend suddenly stopped and sat on the ground.

"… a second … please … breathe …"

Ava sat next to her and tried to decipher the unintelligible words she croaked. She looked around in anticipation and tried to think, knowing that the guards would come any moment. "*What should we do*?" She could not see far for the smoke and her mind did not operate as it used to. A few cars passed and their bright lights barrelled down the street through the smoke. She could hear screams and shouts everywhere. A few metres away, a man was leaning against a flickering streetlight next to them, wretchedly coughing and heaving, his body bent nearly in half. Some people ran past them and immediately something whizzed over their heads and an explosion went off in front of them. It was another tear gas container that hit the ground right next to them. There was more smoke. Trying to overcome her panic attack, Ava grabbed her friend by the arm and pulled her up.

"Come on girl! We should keep going."

"I can't … my side!"

"Come on! You can do this. We've got to run or we'll die. They are after us."

Ava made her friend run for a few more blocks, but they were running too slow. They needed to find a way out or the police guards would catch them. She desperately looked around to find the entrance of a side street but to no avail. The government militia forces behind them were randomly shooting at the crowd to disperse the protesters and break down the demonstration. The The menacing sound of gunfire could be heard from everywhere. The shots were mostly aimless, and no one knew for sure in which direction the police guards aimed their guns, but several times, the sound of a gunshot was followed by the terrified shouts of the people. For the first time in her life, Ava was terrified. *"Think, think, think!"* She had to find a way out.

They continued stumbling along, both dizzy with fear and weariness and unable to breathe properly. A group of protesters were running towards them from behind. Two men were helping an injured boy, trying to carry him to a safe place. The boy was very young and in a serious condition. Ava stopped to look at them. By then, her friend was sobbing.

"I can't go on! I can't breathe!"

Suddenly, a blue pickup truck appeared in the street and stopped beside them. Its window was rolled down a little. Someone from the passenger seat, his green band fastened around his wrist, called them. "Bring the boy here! Put him in!"

People ran and brought the injured boy closer to the truck. A man who was sitting in the truck tray grabbed the boy by his arm and lifted him into the truck and the boy screamed in pain. Other people hurriedly went up there, too. Ava pushed her friend close to the truck. It took all her breath to shout a few words.

"Please let us in! My friend cannot walk anymore."

Someone pulled Ava's friend in. Ava jumped up after her and heaved her body over. Soon the truck started to move, went over the median into the opposite lane, headed towards the guards and somehow passed through them. Ava looked back. The guards disappeared in the smoke. Ava sat straight and, even with the fire in her lungs, took a deep breath of relief, "*We are safe. Well, at least for now.*"

The injured boy was lying on the truck tray, bending his knees and breathing fast. He looked around thirteen. His shirt was covered in blood. He coughed and then he pressed his chest and sobbed. Someone sat next to him and put his head on his lap. But nobody knew how to help him further. They hoped the truck would take him to a hospital. Another young man in the truck tray was also wailing, and his friend explained to everyone that he had rinsed his eyes with water, not knowing that it made the tear gas sting even more.

"Before I had a chance to tell him not to do it, he poured his bottled water onto his eyes and immediately screamed in pain. There was nothing I could do except dragging him away immediately. Guardsmen were beginning to charge on the crowd, swinging their clubs."

Ava's friend was feeling very sick. Every two minutes, she turned her head out and threw up in the street. A man in a grey shirt handed Ava a dampened handkerchief.

"Here. Put it against her nose and tell her to breathe through it. It'll help."

Ava put the handkerchief against her own nose first. It gave her a small amount of relief. Then she put it against her friend's nose and mouth and asked her to breathe slowly. The truck was moving fast with its head lamps off. The injured boy moaned at the truck's every motion. Then, all at once, the truck jumped in the air and stopped with a sudden halt. The injured boy let out a howl of anguish and rolled in agony. The driver and the man in the passenger seat stepped out and ran to look. Some other people also stepped down the tray to see what had happened. Whatever it was, it did not seem good.

"Shit!"

Ava looked around with a churning stomach. She was not familiar with this part of the city and did not know where they were. But she knew that they had to go. If they walked far enough, there was a chance to be out of the guards' reach.

Ava looked at her friend. Tears and snot were dripping down her face. The handkerchief was soaked and could not be used further. Ava held her friend's hand and pushed it hard. There was no other way. They had to be strong at least for a few more hours.

"We should go. Come on! Be brave! We'll find a way out."

Ava's friend nodded. They stepped down the truck tray and started to walk in the street. They could see people here and there, walking or running. There was no sign of the police guards. If only they could walk to a main street free from guards, they had a chance to find a taxi or take the bus to go home. Their hope did not last long, though. Soon a group of people ran past them. The young man with the brown cap was among them.

"Run! Run! They are after us. They are close!"

Ava could not say anything. They simply could not run. Seeing Ava's friend in that miserable condition, the man slowed down and offered to carry her on his back. They saw a tall man who was helping another woman to stand up from the ground. The woman had a green scarf around her neck and was crying. They all continued to half-run half-walk to a side street. The swarm guards had started to shoot at people again and the sound of bullets echoed in the narrow street.

"Come on! This way! Walk faster!"

The man with the brown cap led them forward as if he knew the place. Suddenly, the woman with the green scarf collapsed on the ground. She could not continue walking even with the help of the tall man. Everyone stopped. The man with the cap put Ava's friend on the ground and ran towards the houses in the street. He ran, knocked on the doors with his fist and asked for help. Ava sat next to the woman and tried to soothe her with gentle words. She rubbed her back while looking behind to see if the police guards were coming. The tall man looked overwrought. A small crowd entered the street and frantically looked at them.

"They are coming this way. Run!"

Ava knew that they could not run any further. Her heart was beating fast, "*What to do?*" She was so frustrated that she was at the verge of tears Then, out of the blue, one of the doors opened and the head of an elderly man appeared. He looked around restlessly and motioned them to come in.

"In here. Hurry!"

Ava helped her friend up and walked hastily toward the door. With an enormous effort, the young man with the cap pulled the woman with the green scarf and helped her walk. A few other people followed them and rushed inside and the elderly man quickly closed the door. He gestured to everyone to be quiet.

"Shhh! They are coming!"

Ava was panting heavily from running. She put her hands over her mouth, trying to quiet her breathing. Everybody was dead quiet. In a few seconds, footsteps were heard. Black helmeted and plain clothed riot police merged into the street and, for no good reason, started to smash parked car windows with their batons. Ava could hear their radios crackled with rough messages. One of them fired his gun into the air and shouted at people that if they did not keep away from their windows, they would be responsible for their own lives.

When the street was quiet and the police guards were gone, Ava let out a breath she did not realise she was holding and looked around. They were in a small hallway leading to a staircase at the top of which a child stood in light yellow pyjamas. With wide eyes and an open mouth, the child was looking at Ava's friend who had gone on a coughing fit. Ava smiled at her when she was setting her friend on the stairs. Other protesters also hesitantly began to sit on the steps one by one.

To Ava, everything was still blurry. Her eyes were nearly numb from burning and she had to blink fast to ease the burn. The tall man was also injured. His forehead, right above the eyebrow, was bleeding. When he took off his T-shirt to put it on his forehead, his breath became fast and laboured and he bit his lips. Ava saw that his side was purple looking and remembered, with respect and admiration, what the man did for the woman with the green scarf. He almost carried her for quite a long distance despite his severe condition.

The man with the brown cap came to Ava and suggested he help Ava's friend. He took a cigarette from his pocket and flicked a lighter. It took him three goes to light up the cigarette as his hands were shaking. He inhaled deeply on his cigarette and blew out the smoke to Ava's friend's face. Ava looked at the cigarette glowing red and eating away its white paper. Her mind was empty and for once she was not thinking about anything.

Ava's friend was still coughing and crying. The man with the cap stared at her for a second then turned his head and sighed out his nose. A woman came down the stairs from one of the apartments and offered help. She took Ava's friend and the woman in the green scarf to her apartment to wash their faces and refresh. She said that she would bring some milk for others to soothe their throats. The child in yellow pyjamas followed them to the apartment. The man with the cap then came to Ava and blew smoke into her red and sore eyes. Ava looked at the thin grey cloud of smoke that hovered in front of her face and slowly dissolved. Her throat burnt and breathing was torture, but the smoke helped a bit.

The elderly man was still standing at the door to monitor what was happening in the street. People took turns explaining what they experienced. The tall man, who was helping the woman with the green scarf, was talking excitedly. His voice was quiet and croaky.

"They had pistols and high voltage clubs. I saw with my own eyes that some of them used shotguns. From where we were hiding, we could see a boy who fell on the ground after being hit by one of those shotguns at close range. His fall triggered a stampede on the sidewalk. There were more tear gas grenades and smoke filled the air. We could hear glass shattering. The guards walked and mercilessly destroyed everything on their way. Hiding was no longer an option, so we decided to run; but no matter how fast we ran, the sound of bullets got closer. The plainclothes riot police on motorbikes attacked people. If I hadn't seen it with my own eyes, I'd never believe this could happen. They laid into the crowd with their truncheons, knocking people to the ground. They severely beat everyone they could reach. And there were vans. They grabbed and took people in them. I saw a man who was dragged off and a woman who was still shouting at them even as she was being clubbed down."

The woman came back from her apartment with a few cartons of milk. The tall man walked to her and took one. He drank some, coughed and sputtered, waited for the coughing to stop and drank some more. Ava also took a packet of milk for herself and drank some. The relief came in seconds. She coughed and sipped some more milk. Then, she held the milk in her mouth for a few seconds before swallowing it, trying to douse the flames in her chest. She then moved towards the man with the cap and offered him the packet of milk. He was sitting on the floor holding his knees against his chest.

"Thanks!"

The man muttered a few other unintelligible words to her before coughing. His voice was quiet and low and Ava did not understand what he said. But she nodded and sat on the stairs next to him. After drinking milk, the protesters were clearly in better conditions. They started to talk to one another and tried to help those who were injured. Ava listened to a woman who was talking to the elderly man.

"People did not give up. We scattered, but soon regrouped in another street. But as soon as we resumed our protest, a line of armoured camionnettes and personnel carriers with machine gun tarots entered from a side street. We didn't expect that. Some kind people went around and helped where they could. Some others, like you, did other small acts of generosity and left the doors of their houses open so that protesters could enter and hide from the police. In some small alleys that were free from riot police, people managed to burn fires with papers and broken wooden boxes to help neutralise the effects of teargas."

The elderly man listened and nodded. The woman was trying to relate the brave stories, but her voice shivered. Ava, the man in the cap and some others who were sitting on the stairs, silently listened, too. Ava's talkative nature urged her to join the conversation, but she did not have the breath. Soon, Ava's friend and the woman with the green scarf came back. They looked much better. Their red puffy faces showed the aftereffects of tear gas, but they could visibly breathe more easily. The woman had her green scarf around her waist and carried a tray with a jar of cold water and some glasses. People each took a glass of water each. The icy water revived them all.

It was time to go. The street seemed very still. The elderly man opened the door and looked out. No one was out there. The refugees thanked the elderly man and exited the house one by one. Ava and her friend along with the man with the cap, the tall man and the woman with the green scarf formed a group and left the house together. They walked silently through several small streets. At the end of a narrow alley, they passed a few people who were still sitting next to an almost extinguished fire. They exchanged looks. A young boy with red swollen eyes smiled at them.

"It is the end of them. We stand strong together. We'll never give up. We'll never be quiet. We will win."

Everyone confirmed with either words or nods. Ava was tired and in pain, but the devotion and determination in the eyes of the young boy warmed up her heart. She held her friend's hand and pressed it.

"We shall overcome!"

Eight

Public protests continued for many more days during which some people were fatally shot and thousands were arrested. The demonstrations, however, became sporadic due to the shootings and mass arrests. Riot police were stationed in the main squares and intersections of populous cities in the country. The motionless masked men stood in lines, like an impenetrable wall, holding their shields and rifles in front of them. No one was allowed to stand in the street and talk to another person for more than a few minutes. No one was allowed to approach the guards. Even if a passerby stopped somewhere to tie their shoelaces, they were immediately warned to keep moving. The internet was significantly slowed down, and access to social media platforms, as well as the ability to send and receive text messages, was restricted by the government. The country was under military rule, and prohibition was in force. Fear had engulfed many people, especially in large cities.

Then, the government police started to arrest people from their homes and crushed the protesters one by one. They conducted investigations to recognise people from the random videos taken by mobile phones in the demonstrations and shared on social media. In a series of raids across the city, the police arrested a huge number of people. Some of those arrested were people who did not even take part in the protests. They were merely in the street for various reasons, such as returning home from their workplace or from shopping. Some said that they had never been in the streets, and the police had just made a mistake in their investigation. Most of those who were taken into custody were sentenced to many years in jail and lashed in sham courts, without having access to a fair trial or even to a lawyer.

The number of detainees was so high that the existing prisons soon became full, and new areas were assigned for keeping those who were arrested. The detainees had to stay in the prison while waiting their interrogation. These makeshift prisons were in terrible condition. Cells were overcrowded. Sometimes, there was no space to lie down. Sometimes, people held in custody were not allowed to go to the bathroom, and they had to relieve themselves in the very room they were kept in. Food was scarce, and when available, it was of bad quality. And those who were injured did not receive any medical attention.

Those who eventually came out of the prison related horrifying stories of what they experienced during interrogation. Many of those who were arrested were inhumanly tortured both physically and emotionally. Most of them were brutally beaten. Some were put in solitary confinement. There were those who were held in small windowless cells with radiators on during hot days and a wide ceiling lamp on 24/7. The police put the detainees under pressure and forced them to confess and name other people or intimidated them into televised confessions by threatening to kill them or harm their families. The point of these confessions was not so much to incriminate but to humiliate, to make people complicit in their own subjugation. If these prison walls had mouths, they could not stop telling the untold stories of the atrocities they witnessed.

"They took my brother and me for a drive. We were tied up, blindfolded, and gagged. They took us to an isolated area. There was no sound. Nobody talked. And then, they shot something. I was certain they had shot my brother. I tried to scream, but I could not. It took me a week to realise that my brother was still alive ..."

"They took us to the gallows, made us stand on metal stools and put the ropes around our necks. Then they kicked the stools. We fell. For more than a minute, none of us realised that the ropes were not tied to anything ..."

"Someone in the room had asthma. He did not feel well in the crowded room and begged to be taken to the hospital or be provided with some medicine. They ignored him for the whole day. He was unconscious, and his face was the colour of purple when they took him out. We never knew if he lived..."

There were also stories of lashing and raping, of bloodstains on shirts and pants, of bruised faces, torn muscles, polluted wounds, and shattered skins. Some talked about the detainees being injected with chemicals that temporarily paralysed them. And there were silent stories that even the walls would feel shame to retell.

The city was flooded with fear. Most people walked around with their heads down and shoulders caved in. Terrified parents encouraged their children to avoid conflict with government forces. But despite the arrests, the investigations, the tortures, and the presence of riot police everywhere in the city, there were those – like Ava and some of her friends – who continued their small acts of resistance.

Ava felt she could not be frightened by anyone in the world. Demonstrations in the city streets gave her a sense of power that was almost ethereal. Her safety had become her parents' utmost concern. The father shouted and cursed. Even her mother had set aside her distanced behaviour and tried to dissuade Ava from what she was doing, reasoning that she would fall victim to complacency. But Ava refused to conform. She was surely an idealist. To her mother's directions, she boldly stated that she had a mountain to climb and that she was going to jolly well reach the top or die in the attempt.

Nevertheless, Ava's audacious acts of resistance did not last long. Ava and some of her friends were among those who were recognised in a published video. The government police started an investigation on them and soon found their whereabouts. They were all arrested about a month after the election day, putting an end to the 'climb'.

Nine

I cannot breathe
My forehead is flaming hot
I cannot see a thing
My eyes are blindfolded

I am trapped
They have fenced me in
I am broken
They have beaten me up

My brain aches
Foul thoughts in my mind
My insides heave
Vile taste in my mouth

Gruff voices and rough hands
I hate these stinking men
The darkness swallows me
I feel the spinning in my head

I cower, I shrink
I am choking, dying
I wail in anguish
My ears are throbbing

"Give me names and I will let you go!"
A calligraphy of names in absence of images fills my head …

Now I know what it is to be devastated
I have learned the secret of suffering
Now I know why my father cursed
I have identified pain

I wipe the names from my mind
So as to appear scatterbrained
I hold myself tight
So as not to scream

Ten

The father is in a wide, dark hall with sombre red benches attached to the walls. It is heaving with people who sit at tables, eating and talking. The father looks at them, but all the faces are blurry behind a thick fog. He goes closer to see and to sit on a bench with them, but he darts back, horror-struck. People at the tables are not talking … they are moaning. Most of them are mutilated. Some have their guts spilled out. A strange sound of laughter comes from the profound shadow at the end of the hall. The father scampers towards the end, but no matter how many steps he takes, the end of the room stays as far. He looks towards the end of the hall and sees a man dressed in red with a glowing iron in hand. '*They are burning someone,*' the father thinks. He increases his pace and runs faster. A young girl lets out a wail that echoes through the hall. 'It's Ava … They are burning her …' The father still runs, but everywhere is pitch black. He shouts as loud as he can, "Avaaaaa!" but his cry is carried through the darkness and falls into the folds of quiet. He opens his mouth to cry out again …

The father shouted and woke up with a racing heart, breathing heavily. He was sleeping on the living room sofa, and the room was pitch-black. It was a hot night, and the father was moist with sweat. It took him a good five seconds to realise where he was and what had happened.

"Nightmare! … It was a bloody nightmare!" he mumbled.

Nightmares were not new to the father. They had been happening to him for years and regularly disturbed his sleep. The tossing and turning dreams disturbed him almost every night, but he did not get used to them. They felt so real, so profound, so concrete … scaring him to death. Every single time, he woke up shaking with shortness of breath and pounding heartbeats. Nightmares had always been a distressing experience, but they had never been that dreadful. They were loathsome living creatures that could read his mind and attack his most vulnerable weak point.

"These nightmares should come to an end! I need to find a way to stop them."

The father was not feeling well. He was stupefied when he found out Ava was arrested. He had shouted and cursed until he lost his voice, and punched the wall with his fists until his knuckles bled and his hands were numb. Then dark thoughts attacked his mind like knives, cutting and slicing his soul into pieces, making him unable to feel anything or think properly. Two sleepless nights had passed, and on the third, when sleep eventually came, the nightmares were there waiting for him.

The father wiped the sweat off his face with a tissue, went to the kitchen, poured some vodka into a glass, and knocked it back in two swallows. He then started to pace the house back and forth, trying to think. Soon he found himself in Ava's room. He turned on the light and walked in. The unmade bed, the open book on the bedside table, the papers and colourful pens on the desk, the cassette player and cassettes on the shelf, the posters on the wall, and the blue curtain wafted in the warm breeze coming from the open window caused a million butterflies to flutter in his stomach and a million memories to flood his mind.

The father remembered a day, long ago when he had lost Ava on a busy street. She was about five years old then. The father had told her to stay close while he was buying books from a book stall and not to wander. When he had turned around and not been able to see Ava, his heart had literally stopped beating. He had gone in circles searching for her, madly shouting her name. It had taken him ten whole minutes to find her in front of a spice shop a hundred metres away. He had grabbed her arm and shaken her hard, shouting. Ava had cried. She had not expected the severe reaction. She had not even known she had been lost.

"Yes, I overreacted. But she didn't understand. I thought I had lost her …"

The father was speaking loudly to himself. His voice echoed in the dead silent room. He then remembered that he and Ava had indeed had a good relationship with each other before. She thought of him as the strongest and wisest man in the world. He read books to her or asked Ava to read to him. Ava could read and write since she was only five years old. And when she was older, he had taught her to interpret poetry, to analyse historical events, and to play chess and backgammon. They spent many hours together every day. He was so proud of her.

The father walked toward the bookshelf. The children's books he had bought Ava when she was a kid were still there. He brushed his fingers over the collections of *The Adventures of Tintin* and *Good Stories for Good Children*. Like magic, his fingertips made life to thousands of memories from the past. On top of the children's books, some others were horizontally stacked. He randomly took one of the books and opened it on a random page. It was the story of 'Seven Steel Boots and Seven Steel Sticks.' The familiar words soothed the father, and he sat on Ava's bed to read the story.

Once upon a time, there was a King who had three daughters. When it was time for the girls to marry, the King asked all the young men in the kingdom to march in from the palace. Each girl had a red apple in their hands. The custom was that they had to throw their apples at any man they liked and then they would marry them. The two older girls threw their apples at two rich courtiers, but when the younger girl threw her apple, the apple fell on the ground and rolled down the road to the top of a snake's nest.

The girl was very troubled, but there was no other choice. She had to marry the snake. That night, after the sunset, the snake instantaneously became a very handsome young man. He told the young princess that he was an enchanted prince who was cursed by an evil witch to be a snake in the morning and a man at night. His name was Malek.

The princess soon fell in love with her husband, and the young couple was living happily together. One night, the King invited all his daughters and their husbands to dinner. Everybody expected the young princess to come with a snake and were surprised when they saw her next to an attractive young man. The sisters were the most curious, and the princess told them the story of her husband. The sisters told her that it is not honourable for a princess to live with a snake. The oldest sister told her to burn her husband's snakeskin at night so that he could not become a snake again in the morning.

That night, when Malek was in his room, the princess sneakily took the snakeskin and threw it in the fireplace. As soon as the skin burnt, Malek ran out of the room and screamed out of agony. He told the princess that now he had to go back to the evil witch and live with her for the rest of his life. The princess was heartbroken. She told her husband that she was so regretful and asked him if there was any way to save Malek, "I would do anything to atone for what I have done!"

Malek, however, told her that it was an impossible task, "I am now a prisoner of the witch, and she lives too far away. No one can walk far enough to find her place. I have heard that the only way to accomplish such a journey is to have seven steel boots and seven steel sticks. One would walk on until all the boots are worn out and all the walking sticks are broken." With tears in his eyes, Malek left the house, and as soon as he set foot outside, he disappeared into thin air.

The princess cried for forty days and forty nights. She had realised that she could not live without her beloved husband. So, she decided to walk on the impossible path. She went to her father's palace and asked the King's armourer to make seven steel boots and seven steel sticks for her. She then said farewell to her father and her sisters and with valiant dreams and a heart full of fire began what seemed an insurmountable journey, determined to find the witch's enchanted castle.

The princess walked for seven years. She walked until her boots were worn, and the sticks were all broken. But eventually, after she forced a way through the thick brier hedge around the witch's castle, she found what she was looking for. Upon entering the castle, she encountered a skinny dog and a scrawny horse chained to the wall. There were a batch of bones in front of the horse and a pile of hay in front of the dog. She put the bones in front of the dog and the hay in front of the horse. Then she entered a hall with numerous doors. Some of the doors were open, and some were closed. She opened all the closed doors and closed all the open ones. She then went down a long staircase and found Malek in chains in a cold and dark and musty cell in the dungeon.

Malek was flabbergasted and overjoyed to see the princess. He wanted to ask her how she could find him. But the princess knew that they did not have much time. She unlocked the chains with her hairpin, and the husband and wife ran out of the dungeon. Suddenly, the evil witch woke up and saw the young couple running. She ordered the previously closed doors to get them. But the doors said, "Why should we get them? You left us closed for so long, and she opened us!" The witch ordered the previously opened doors to get them. But they said, "Why should we get them? You left us open for so long, and she closed us!" She ordered the dog to get them. But the dog said, "Why should I get them? You gave me hay, and she gave me bones!" The witch ordered the horse to get them. But the horse said, "Why should I get them? You gave me bones, and she gave me hay!"

So, the princess and Malek could run away from the evil witch. They soon settled in a nearby town and lived there together happily ever after. In their happy life, Malek often asked the princess how she could find him, and the princess told him that when there is love, nothing is impossible.

The father remembered reading the story to Ava several times. One day, after the story was finished, Ava had asked the father if he would come to find her if an evil witch put a spell on her and took her away. He had laughed and told her that first he had to find an armourer to make him seven steel boots and seven steel sticks.

The father turned the pages of the book. Before the next story began, he found a picture of a boat on a vast sea. The image reminded him of the time he was in the Navy, and as thoughts often ramble, he remembered the time when the majestic sight and sound of the flat ocean filled his young self with wonder. The time when he rose way before dawn in the morning to catch the bronze-flecked sun easing up over the shimmering water. The time when having a glass of vodka was a pleasure, not a necessity. The time of music and dance and laughter and being carefree.

"I've messed up my life."

The father closed the book and put it on the bedside table. He walked the length of the room and leaned his forehead on the window. The moon rolled out from behind thick clouds and bleached the world with an eerie whiteness. He looked at a stray cat crossing the street towards the big trashcan to find food. A green piece of cloth that was clinging to the trashcan attracted his attention. The father turned back and brought his fist down on the dressing table with such strong force that the brush and all the pins fell on the floor. He touched his throat to ease the lump and noticed that his body was burning hot.

"I've badly messed up my life."

He had forgotten his identity as a father. He had to take that identity back. He would take his daughter out of prison. It was time to put on his 'steel boots'.

Eleven

"Wait outside!"

The security guard shouted at people and pushed them back forcefully. Some lost their balance and stumbled. The father was among those who fell. The building was full of parents, siblings, aunts, and uncles who had come to ask about the whereabouts of their arrested family members. They had been standing there for hours, waiting to be called in and to ask questions, but no one could go inside the office yet. Apparently, those who worked in custodial services were not in a hurry to give answers. Now the security was shoving them and forcing them to leave the building and wait outside.

Unaccustomed to being kept waiting and being assaulted, the furious and overtired father marched out of the building, walked to a tree, and hit the tree trunk with his fist. The physical pain helped him forget about his distress for a second. For many years, he was always the one responsible for other people's irritation. He was the one who ridiculed and offended people. Now he was tasting his own medicine, and he realised it was bitter. The worst part was that he was unable to retort. He had to stay quiet and was surprised that he had the capacity to throw away his pride and tolerate the humiliation that had become the new normal in his life.

The father had begun his quest with exuberance. He was hopeful, full of energy, and excitement, when he started searching wide and long for Ava. He had begun by going to different prisons to discover where his daughter was kept. He had gone first to all the known places, everywhere he knew, and when he could not find Ava in any of those, he started to search for her in all the 'unknown' places. At night, he wrote Ava's name and date of birth on small pieces of paper. In the mornings, he gave what he called 'pursue papers' to people who worked in police headquarters and prisons and bribed them to find some information about her. During the day, and for long hours, the father sat outside the buildings waiting for the doormen, porters, or janitors in the buildings to come with an answer. He begged for information from every security force in the police stations. Some took pity and tried to help, but many sneered at him when they saw his helplessness and ineffectuality. Evidently, they took pleasure in tormenting desperate parents.

After the security guards threw everyone out, they closed and barred the entrance. The father had grown weary. He had hurt his right leg and ankle in the crowd crush, and his right hand after he hit the tree trunk. His heart had generated a nervous palpitation and he was trembling all over. His stomach twisted and made him nauseous. The pain and humiliation were beyond his tolerance, and tears of helplessness involuntarily appeared in his eyes. He had not cried since forever. The uncontrolled crying took him aback. He took a deep breath, wiped his tears with his clenched injured fist, and leaned against the tree in front of the building. It was another shimmering hot day with no breeze. He had not eaten anything since morning, was hungry and thirsty, and longed for a glass of vodka.

The heat had made everyone tetchy and irritable. Some of the parents decided to leave. A woman who still could think clearly started to make a list. She wrote the names of all those who decided to stay and gave the list to the security. The father had no choice but to wait until his name was called. He looked around and consciously saw the other parents for the first time. They were all consumed with worry, anxiety, and stress. Some of them were talking about what they had to go through to find their children. The father listened and nodded at their familiar stories. He had been through those paths. He had asked for help from anyone who could have an influence on the judiciary committee. A woman, who was sitting on the curb, was explaining how she had to bribe the officeholders everywhere she had been to. The father knew well about that, as well. He too had bribed all sorts of people in the past days, high and low. In his quest, he had soon discerned that bribing is the key to unlock mouths and doors. This was the country where bribery could do anything, he thought, and he was grateful that he was well-supplied with money. But the prices were high, and although the father was well-off, a big part of his savings had already been wiped.

The father waited for three hours before he was eventually called in. He made a move towards the building, but tormented by hunger, thirst, fatigue, and pain, and feeling pins and needles in his ankles, he could barely walk. The security guard guided him to a door at the end of a long narrow corridor and told him to wait for the person inside to come out. The father sat on the only chair there and, waiting for time to pass, counted all the closed doors in the corridor. Then, he fixed his eyes on a small window that was open to warm air and tried to disperse the negative thoughts that filled his head, *"the princess opened all the closed doors and closed all the open ones."*

When it was his turn to go in, the father made every attempt to compose himself. He knocked and opened the door. In the office, a bearded man with a horrible body odour was sitting at a filthy desk. The foul smell in the room was so revolting that the father could not help but grimace. *"Here at last, I am in the witch's lair!"* he thought and swallowing an urge to retch stepped inside and closed the door behind him. The bearded man was rapidly writing something in a notebook and did not even raise his head to look at the father. He intentionally made the father stand there for a few minutes before he eventually looked at him and rudely addressed him with a question.

"Who are you looking for?"

The father looked at the man's dead flat eyes, took one of the pursue papers out of his pocket, and handed it to him. The bearded man read the paper, turned to a new page in his notebook, and copied the information on the paper. Then, he sat back and began to ask more detailed questions: the father's name and age, his address and phone number, and his jobs in the past twenty years. He also asked all sorts of questions about Ava's private life: where she studied, what her hobbies were, with whom she spent time, if she had a boyfriend. The father answered all his questions with a bitter feeling of abjection. The bearded man wrote the responses in his notebook and commented on them using abusive words.

"These dirty scumbags! These nasty bastards! They deserve whatever's coming to them and worse."

After each comment, the father's face flushed, and his heart thumped. But he had to swallow his rage, quietly listen to all those insults and scornful remarks, and nod his head. He was literally going through hell and forced himself to keep going. He was resentful at the way he was treated and despised the stinky bearded man. He desperately longed for being able to stifle the monster with some grudging answers he had in his mind.

Since the beginning of his search for Ava, the father's behaviour and attitude had immensely changed. He had found a way to control his emotions. On that day and in that office, standing in front of that insolent man, the father showed a totally different version of himself. Although he was inflamed inside, his demeanour did not reveal his state of mind, and he abased himself to the greatest extent possible.

The father was petrified at the thought of Ava having to stay in prison for a longer time, so he apologised for his daughter's misconduct and begged for forgiveness. And eventually, when the time was right, the father told the bearded man that he would "do anything" for him to tell where Ava was, forgive her, and find a way to release her. He used the power of his imagination to see the situation as a strategy game and called for his old negotiation skills. He changed his position from the unfamiliar stance of being oppressed to the familiar intelligent contriver. He brought forward the strongest arguments to manipulate the greedy man. And to conclude, he repeated his words.

"I would do anything!"

As if under a spell, the bearded man looked beyond the father's face at his fantastic long-lost treasure. He picked his nose delicately with his index finger while contemplating.

"It's costly!"

Trying to shake off the disgust, the father concentrated on the evil sparkle in the stinky man's eyes and faintly smiled. Knowing that he had him, he took a deep breath and strove to respond with as much coolness as he could manage.

"It shouldn't be a problem."

The bearded man took an empty bag of potato chips and dug the salt and grease out of the corner with the same finger he used to pick his nose. Then, he motioned to the father to sit down on one of the rusty iron chairs in the room. The father took another deep breath, "Checkmate!" The pain in his ankle did not bother him any longer. He did not even feel hungry or thirsty. He firmly walked the three steps towards the chair and sat down holding his head high with pride. The bearded man suddenly stood up and rushed out of his office.

"I will see if they can bring us some tea."

The father nodded. The way the bearded man hurried out of the room reminded the father of the famous stage direction in Shakespeare's *The Winter's Tale* and brought a smile to his face, *"Exit, pursued by a bear!"*

Twelve

The process of rescuing Ava was more strenuous than the father thought. After his discussion with the stinky bearded man, the father still had to go to many other places, encounter several other officeholders, and endure more humiliations. And, as if the insults he endured during the day was not enough, humiliations haunted him in abstract forms in his gruesome nightmares. He had to find a lawyer who convinced Ava to sign papers where she confessed to the most absurd crimes that she had never committed, promised not to conduct such acts again, and beseeched forgiveness. The official's thirst for money was not easily quenched either. In the following days after meeting the bearded man, the father had to sell both his car and the apartment they were living in. He sold them at a highly reduced price as he urgently needed the money and had no other way of securing it quickly. He had to undergo many more ups and downs of the existing bureaucracy until, eventually, with the help of money and connections, he bought Ava's freedom. It cost him all his interior dignity, his pride, and his lifetime savings. Nevertheless, all his efforts, torments, and agonies were paid off the moment the father saw Ava walk out of the prison building.

The father had not been able to sleep the night before, or maybe he did not want to sleep to avoid foreboding dreams. So, he had decided to take a taxi and go to prison before dawn when it was still dark. He stood in front of the prison door on the other side of the street and leaned against the wall. Beyond and above the prison building, he watched the sun rise blazing and bright, and listened to the sound of trees rustling in the wind and the birds singing to the sunrise. The scenery brought back buried heart-warming memories from another world long ago. The father smiled and fixed his gaze at the prison door, waiting for it to be opened.

It took a few hours until Ava finally came out. When the prison guard opened the door, the father watched her step out of the dark corridor. She had a loose scarf on her head, and her long heavy hair was falling about her narrow shoulders. To the father, she looked more beautiful than ever, thanks to the fevered flush of her cheeks. He slowly walked towards her, trying to absorb and retain every moment of delight in his heart. He took each step consciously and was completely mindful of Ava's features. He could see the tears that welled up in her eyes and her lips that curved to a warm but shaky smile. She did not look away while the father was approaching. The father's lips were moving.

"This is me!"

Ava blinked to clear the tears in her eyes and did her best to meet her father's eyes. He had become an old man. Ava noticed that he had lost weight, and his face was much more lined than before. There were new creases above and below his lips, as well as at the corners of the mouth. His forehead was also scored with new lines that arched one above the other, following the arches of the eyebrows, and there were new radiating lines about his eyes. His face was worn, his hair was grey, and his pain was palpable. But Ava could clearly see a trace of the man she knew a long time ago.

The father stretched his hand and brushed a lock of her hair with his fingers. He thumbed her tears away and then closed his arms tight around her. Ava embraced him back rapidly. They stayed in each other's arms for what seemed like forever. For Ava, at that moment, her father was the emblem of both peace and strength. There was only safety and comfort in leaning against him, the wonder of the protecting circle of his arms, and the feeling of complete refuge and reassurance. She could feel the absolute serenity created by her father's might. For the father, there was transcendental joy, a load of relief, and a great amount of love in his heart. He had found his little girl and saved her from the evil witch.

Ava came back home with her father after sixty-three days of imprisonment. She was weary and broken. The father was also drained, but he felt like a succeeder.

That night, the father went to bed untroubled, quickly drifted away, and slept without nightmares for the first time in years. Instead of nightmares, he dreamed that he was standing in a vast desert watching the sunrise in the east, but when he turned around, he saw yet another sun rising from the west. The wind was in his face. Light was glimmering. Far, far away, in the south, the clouds could be dimly seen as remote grey shapes. There were two suns in the sky, and he could feel the warmth of both washing the cold of the desert night off him. It was the most beautiful scene he had ever seen in his life. When he woke up, the father found himself engulfed in a wave of absolute calm. The dream filled him

with a peculiar joy that he carried about with him for the rest
of his life.

Thirteen

"Have you started to pack?"

The English teacher was among the few friends who came to visit Ava after she was released from prison. Many of Ava's friends were still detained, and Ava had not contacted her other friends because she did not want to put them at risk. People who were discharged from prison were under scrutiny, and those who contacted them could be later investigated and arrested. The English teacher had called Ava's mother every single day when she had found out that Ava was arrested, and as soon as Ava was out, she came to visit her despite the potential peril. Her visit, though, was not like their usual days together.

They were sitting at Ava's desk, where they usually sat when the teacher came for the IELTS classes. The desk looked empty and bare without books, papers, pens, and markers. It looked depressing without the charming Ava on the other side talking, laughing, and telling jokes. Ava had not talked much since the teacher arrived. She had not replied to any of the teacher's questions through words. Ava had immensely changed, both in appearance and demeanour. She had lost weight. Her cheeks were pale, and her previously twinkling eyes had become dim and cloudy. And, she had practically become a silent girl. Her pressed lips not only represented her agony and anger but could showcase her voicelessness. For the first time since they knew one another, the teacher had to take the initiative to keep the conversation going.

"What are you going to take with you? Do you want me to help?"

Ava shook her head. The teacher looked at the two big empty suitcases that were standing beside the wall and transmitted a melancholy shade to the room. The English teacher knew that Ava's parents had sold the apartment and were moving. When she came in, she noticed that nothing was in its place. The empty shelves, the carpetless floors, and the boxes that were sporadically laid out here and there had created a discordant scene. Ava's room, though, had remained untouched. She did not have the heart and energy to look through her belongings and sort out what she wanted to take with her and what she needed to leave.

It was a bleak and greyish afternoon. Throughout the day, huge menacing clouds had thundered into the city and set up camp above it. Not succeeding in communicating with her friend, the English teacher stood up, walked towards the window, and looked at the black sky of the sad afternoon. The sorrowful old song that was being played through the cassette player made the atmosphere even more morose. The teacher thought she could not bear the weight of grief anymore.

"I think I will start to cry now!"

Ava sat straight and almost smiled. For the first time that day, she consciously took notice of the teacher's presence. She stood up, walked to the window, and stood next to her English teacher. They looked at the sky together for some time in silence. Ava was deep in thought again, but after a few minutes, she suddenly started to speak.

"Could I ever be able to move on with my life?"

It was not clear who the question was addressed to. It was highly probable that Ava was talking to herself. The question seemed more rhetorical than inquisitive. It was as if she was expressing her thoughts in the form of interrogative statements. The teacher, however, responded to the question to be able to hold on to the conversation.

"I think you need to give yourself time."

Ava nodded and became silent again. The English teacher held her hand and without directly looking at her asked if she wanted to talk about the prison days. Ava shivered slightly and shook her head.

"It is too difficult!"

But then she did tell the teacher about how she felt and the gruesome nightmares she recently endured. Fixing her gaze on a remote place in the sky, she started to speak in fragments, with faltering lips, attempting to put the words together.

"I'm going through hell and I feel nothing can save me. Nights are the most terrible. There are these streaks of terrifying nightmares. They're too vivid … too much! And when I'm eventually awake, I'm completely puzzled. For a long time, I can't remember where I am or when it is. And I'm sweaty all over my body … and the bed is all wet, too. Then I shiver. All my body shakes for what seems like hours … and I can't breathe."

Ava's voice quivered and deepened as if she was being stifled. She ran her hand through her hair and the English teacher saw that her hand was also shaking. Recalling and relating the nightmare experiences were too painful to be trivialised, so the teacher did not make any comments. Ava was almost weeping.

"I feel overwhelmed … helpless. And I find it difficult to go back to sleep. It is like … I'm always in a state of alertness."

The teacher hugged her close and whispered comforting words in her ears. Then they sat on the bed by the window alongside each other with thought-heavy heads in stillness and silence for the rest of the evening. Their silence was not an embarrassing reticence. It was a comforting one as if both respected each other's private thoughts. The English teacher was the type of person Ava could do that with; they could sit together in silence endlessly.

The night was dark and dreary. The old songs continued to be played. Every half hour, Ava made a short trip to the cassette player, put a new cassette on, and came back to her position on the bed. Ava and the teacher listened to the music and looked at the changing colours of the sky as it turned from grey to dirty orange to leaden and eventually to black. And when Leonard Cohen started to sing his "Dance Me to the End of Love," they cried together. The teacher cried because she was going to lose a close friend. Ava cried because the lyrics were so reflective of the moment.

The English teacher left Ava in the blackness of the night. Ava told her teacher that she would stay in her room and would not accompany her when she was leaving the house. The teacher nodded in understanding. They hugged each other and promised one another to keep in touch. The teacher was worried for Ava but tried her best not to show her concerns.

"Do me a favour and take care of yourself."

The teacher left Ava with a heavy heart, knowing that she would probably never see her again. She tardily walked through the hall towards the apartment door. In the living room, she saw the father who was sitting on the sofa and staring at the turned-off television. A glass of vodka along with an open book was on the table in front of him. The father turned his head to the sound of her footsteps. The teacher smiled and said goodbye. The father said nothing, but the teacher could detect a faint nod towards her. The teacher searched her mind for something to say and found nothing. So, she just nodded back, thinking how limited her means of expression had become.

Fourteen

Ava left the country three days after she was released, not a moment too soon. She eventually packed her suitcases with the help of her mother. She took some of her clothes, a few pairs of shoes, some of her books, her favourite perfume, and a few documents. Most of her personal belongings, though, remained for her parents to decide what to do with them. Ava told them that she did not care if they wanted to dispose of them or donate them. She was certain she did not want them anymore.

Ava's parents' life had turned upside down since the day she was arrested. All the anxiety and agitation they experienced when she was detained, together with losing their life savings and having to sell their apartment, positioned them in a state of precarity and unease. They had to find a place to rent and move away. They anticipated that moving from their familiar place and sending their daughter away would make their life absolutely empty and meaningless.

What followed, however, was not what they expected. In fact, it was not so much of a dire situation. Moving gave them a reason to think less about the past events and the immense emotional pressure they had been under. Somehow, it gave them motivation to carry on. Although what had happened to the family was formidable, a positive change could be detected in Ava's mother. She became more active. She moved around the house, cleaned the rooms, spent more time in grocery stores, bought special ingredients for certain foods, cooked every day and talked to the father more often. She spent hours filling bags, boxes, and suitcases with clothes and other personal items. Packing occasionally gave her an excuse to interact with the father.

'Do you still need this, or should we give it away?'

'Look at this picture in the album. This is when we went to the South to see the Persian Gulf. Oh, how young we were!'

'We can donate these books to the school's library. My sister told me they have bought new shelves at school and are looking for new books suitable for young people.'

'Have you seen the new pizzeria that opened on the corner? How about we order a pizza tonight?'

The father did not understand what made his wife change, but he was surely content about it. When Ava left, he thought that his life would be emptier than ever. Yet, he noticed that the sporadic conversations with his wife could compensate for the absence of his daughter. He stealthily looked at her when she was wandering around the house and for the first time in a long time, he silently praised her beauty. On a few occasions, he even caught her looking at him almost as though she was approving of him. *"Is it because I could take Ava out of prison?"* he wondered. The father did not realise that he had also changed. He still heavily drank every evening but found fewer reasons to lose his temper. Strangely, he had become more tolerant and remained quiet even if he disagreed with or disapproved of someone.

Moving went smoothly after Ava left. In a few months, Ava's parents could rent a small apartment in the suburbs. The apartment was located in a quiet area, away from the chaos of the city and its excessive noise and traffic. The tranquil environment helped the couple to reconcile, and the one-bedroom apartment brought the husband and wife closer to one another.

News from Ava always lifted their spirits. Ava tried her best to continue with her life. She soon settled down in the new country, found a part-time job, and began to study again. In less than a year, she received her IELTS certificate with desirable grades and could commence her studies at the university she had in mind. In one way or another, she managed to recuperate and bounce back.

Fifteen

My dear English teacher,

I've been wanting to call you for so long, but ... well, I am not a phone person anymore. These days I much prefer writing than engaging in conversations. This way, I keep away from long awkward silences that often happen to me every time I try to have a dialogue with someone. So, here I am writing a letter to you. How have you been doing? I truly miss you and your gripping classes. I often catch myself thinking about you and my other friends in Iran. But strangely, the memories seem so remote and unreal.

By the way, I had my IELTS results a couple of months ago. Are you curious to know the scores? Reading 8, Listening 8, Writing 7, Speaking 8. Not bad, huh? And can you guess what my Speaking Question was? You can't believe it. It was to describe an advertisement I disliked! The examiner was surprised by my mixed feelings while I was responding. I had a smile on my face when I first saw the question on the card, then I picked an angry tone when I was talking about the ad and I was almost crying at the end of my short speech! I was thinking about you and our last English class all the time, even though the memory of that day is among the ones I try not to ever recall, considering what happened with my father when you were leaving the house (I am still embarrassed!).

So, as you might have noted, I am trying my best to live my life and act normal, busying myself with university classes and work. I sometimes even try to get to know new people and go to new places. But to tell you the truth, life usually seems so surreal to me. I frequently get confused about where I am and what I am doing. There are still occasional nightmares that leave me panic-stricken. Sometimes, things happen that take me to the past and make me extremely anxious. Sometimes, I spend hours alone, thinking about what has become of me. At such times, I feel detached and separated from this world. But everything is generally OK, and I often find myself interested in what is happening around me. Sometimes I am even motivated and ambitious to change things for the better and make a difference. These are currently the best moments of my life. But they happen very rarely, only when I find an opportunity to help someone, most usually at work.

I've made doing exercises a priority in my life to stay active and to keep myself supple, balanced, and fit. I go either to the gym or the swimming pool every day, and I have recently started to play tennis. I also have a running partner with whom I go jogging on the weekends. But walking is still my favourite sport. Mostly, I walk directionless through the streets for hours on end. I walk amongst the crowds, watch their silent passing, and try to read their stories written on their faces. It seems that everyone has their own battles to fight, and the battles draw their scars on their faces, mostly around the eyes. You, see? I am developing new skills!

I always take a walk to clear my mind and have better feelings, but all the time I find myself thinking about the days after the election. I think about the protests, the arrest, the jail, and wonder if I should have done things differently. In retrospect, however, I still think I made the right moves. Maybe I was a bit too optimistic, but if I went back, I would do this all over again. Or would I? I was put through hell. I went to the underworld, and although I came back alive, I do not want to endure those moments ever again. Do you see my contradictory chain of thoughts? Welcome to the conflicting world of my mind!

There is a nice spot in a park near my house where I often go to read or just have "me time". I usually stay there till sunset. Sitting outside with the sun going down, amongst the changing colours of leaves in different seasons, and feeling the breeze on my face makes the world seem so frivolous and unthreatening. My uneasiness wears off, and all the complications in my mind slip away. I am surprised to see how much resilience there is in human nature. Let the terrible causes for our worst experiences, no matter how scary they were, be removed in any way, and we forget everything and fly back to the first principles of hope and enjoyment. Do you think this is a good thing? I mean forgetfulness. Maybe it is. This should be the key to survival.

Wow! Never before have I written such a long letter. But it feels so good to have someone safe to talk to … I mean to have a monologue with! You have always been a good friend to me. I looked to you for inspiration and I always found it. Whenever I was in a pickle, you helped me out. And you have been an amazing teacher. You could find a way out of every difficult situation through your commitment, your patience, your flexibility, and your sense of humour. Nothing seemed to be a big problem when I was with you.

Do you remember the day you met my father for the first time? I was dying from embarrassment, and you just laughed it off. When we went out, you were on the verge of saying something. Probably, you wanted to ask a question but you thought better of it. You knew how distressed I was, so instead you made a joke about it to make it appear not important. You could always read my mind.

You know? I now think that I judged my father too harshly. These days, many times during the day, I find myself bitter, cynical, and pessimistic. Sometimes I become blunt and tend to ridicule people, and then I remember my father. Many of his biting comments just make sense now. You become resentful when you can't change things that trouble you. They say you can't understand someone until you've walked a mile in their shoes. Well, I think I now understand him better. And perhaps this is the only silver lining in all this mess.

Talking about my father, I remember that I would like to ask you for a favour. I want to send a gift for my father's birthday. One of my university friends is travelling to Tehran next week, and she has accepted to take the gift with her. Surprises had by no means been a common practice in our family, but anyway ... I have decided to surprise my father this year. His birthday is in two months, in May. I am sending it now because I might not find another person who is willing to bring the gift, and I cannot post colognes from here. Can you please go to my parents' place and give it to him for me? I know it means you have to dedicate half of your precious day to me, and I know how you might not feel comfortable seeing my father considering what he might say or do on the day. But you were brave enough to come to our house when I was leaving. So, will you do this, please? I truly have no one else to ask. Thank you so much for always being there for me.

Sending Love,
Ava

Sixteen

"Blow a dandelion and make a wish!"

Ava opened her eyes. Melanie, the little girl Ava was babysitting, was standing in front of her with outstretched arms, offering her a big feathery dandelion. They were in the backyard, enjoying the fine weather and waiting for Melanie's mother to come back. Ava was lying on the hammock on the deck, and Melanie was prancing around and talking to her imaginary friends. It was a peaceful day. Ava looked at the rounded cluster of white hairy seeds and smiled.

"It is so beautiful!"

Melanie giggled and danced away, taking the dandelion with her and scattered the seeds with a strong puff. Ava liked the times she spent with Melanie. She was a smart yet charming girl with a fascinating imagination, easy to deal with and pleasing to have as a companion. They read books and talked for hours about the characters and events in the stories. They watched cartoons together while Melanie nestled in her arm. They watched cartoons over and over again, and every time they laughed so heartily, often uncontrollably, at the funny parts as if they were watching them for the first time. Melanie's favourite game was doing riddles that she either created or found in books, "What is an elephant that is most unrelated to you? – irrelephant!" She could surely put a smile on Ava's face.

Melanie reached the end of the backyard, picked another dandelion and did a handstand against the wall. The dandelion fell out of her hand and a few of its seeds spread across the ground. She quickly placed her feet down and sat on the tall grass that had not been cut for a long time. Then, she picked yet another dandelion, being careful not to damage it.

"Look! It is still April, but most of the dandelions in the garden have changed from suns into moons. Should be warm weather."

Ava looked around the yard. Melanie was right. The white puffballs could be seen everywhere. Melanie ran back to her and pushed the dandelion into Ava's face.

"Blow the dandelion and make a wish. I have already made 5 wishes!"

Ava grabbed the dandelion, closed her eyes, took a deep breath, and blew off the seeds into the air. The seeds were carried over the walls of the small garden by the wind. Ava and Melanie watched them till they disappeared.

"What did you wish for?"

Ava was so lost in thought that it took a minute for her to answer. She looked at Melanie and brushed her hair with her fingers, pulled it away from her face.

"I wished to forget."

Ava's answer sounded dismissive. The peace in her mind had been replaced with an assortment of indistinct memories when she started to wish before she blew the dandelion. She tried to concentrate on the calm swaying that the hammock offered in order to allow a quicker transition to her peaceful state. She also closed her eyes and turned her head to signal the end of the conversation. Melanie, though, never let a conversation die when her curiosity was aroused.

"Forget what?"

Random shots and flashes of scary and painful scenes from the past rushed to Ava's mind. Crushing waves of thoughts ebbed and flowed in her head. The world had suddenly become dark and ghastly.

"Forget everything!"

Melanie widened her eyes in surprise at the answer. She was amazed and seemed thoughtful at the same time. She shook her head.

"Uh-uh! You should not forget everything. You remember Darren? My friend with freckles? Darren's grandma has forgotten everything. Last time I was there, she didn't know me at all. Darren says she doesn't know him anymore, either. She doesn't even know who she herself is. I don't think she is happy."

Dementia. Memory loss and all the confusion associated with it. The inability to recognise familiar places or faces. Ava had not thought about these. Melanie was right, after all.

"Well, then maybe not forget everything, but many things."

Melanie was convinced. She jumped up and clapped her hands. Then raced into the garden again with a new thought in her mind.

"You have to blow a dandelion for each thing you want to forget. I will bring you some."

Ava truly loved this child. She constantly came up with new game ideas. Ava knew that she was looking for an excuse to pick up all the dandelions in the garden. Melanie did not wait for Ava's approval. She picked five or six dandelions meticulously to preserve the seeds and slowly walked back.

"The Little Prince. Do you know him? On his way to Earth, he met someone who drank to forget."

Ava was taken aback. She could vividly hear the sound of ice cubes dropped into a glass and could distinctly smell the repugnant odour of alcohol on the father's breath.

"Actually, I know him too! I mean, I know the Little Prince, but I also know the tippler."

Melanie's face lit up. She cherished pretending games.

"Really? He lives on another planet, doesn't he?"

Ava nodded. She pictured Iran in her head, "Truly another planet!" Melanie carried on with her fantasies.

"He drinks because he wants to forget that he is ashamed. But if I were him, I would try to remember the days when I was proud of myself. If we think about the good things we did, we forget the bad ones."

Ava was stunned by Melanie's words of wisdom. She sat on the hammock, trying to fully digest what Melanie had just said. She looked at the dandelions in Melanie's hands and leisurely separated one from the others.

"For this one then, I will wish for the bad memories to take flight with the seeds and be gone. I wish I will always remember the good things!"

Seventeen

I am recollecting all the memories of the past and trying to organise them. I am trying to remove the black bulky clouds to find the younger me. I am trying to sweep away the alcoholic shadow of a man you had once been. I am recalling the younger you. It is sad that I have to cut through so much dark dense smog to find us. I dig as deep as I can. I plough as far as I can go. I vaguely see my two-year-old self in a yellow dress, running on the lush green grass under the blue sky. I vaguely see a tall, well-built man in whom I find a superhero. It is you; I see your moustache move when you laugh. I like the low and warm sound of your laughter. You are laughing at one of my questions. I am happy that I could amuse you.

Look here! We are in the living room. You are sitting on the ground. I am sitting on your lap. There is a tape recorder and a picture book on the table in front of us. We are recording our voices. I am three years old. I hear your bass voice talking to me and asking me questions. "What is this?" I look at the rooster, but I do not answer your question. You insist, try to encourage me to speak, remind me that our voices are being recorded. "You will listen to your voice later when you grow up." I want to take the initiative. I want to be the one who asks questions. 'What is the rooster doing?' You look at me and smile. 'He crows wake up! Cock a doodle doo!' You mimic the sound of a rooster crowing, waving your arms around as if you are trying to fly. I chuckle. I find the new game gripping. I turn the page. 'What is the cat doing?'

Look there! We are at a bookstore. It is cold. We both have woollen jackets on. We walk through the shelves, take random books, and read random pages. We take our time. We have all the time in the world. I am four years old. I am feeling happy. I like being in the bookstore. I stand on my toes to reach a book on the top shelf. I find a book about space and the stars. The colourful pictures are so cool! Something in the book attracts my attention. I walk towards you and ask you to explain about it. You take the book from me. I look at you reading the page to get familiar with the context. I like looking at you reading. I patiently wait for your answer. I am certain you know the answer. You know all the answers.

Ah! You probably remember this one. We are standing upright, facing one another. Strauss' Blue Danube is played on. I am five years old. You take my hands in yours and bow. We count together, "one, two, three, one, two, three, and move our feet the way you showed me a minute ago. Step your left foot forward. Land softly to give the step a light airy feel. Now step your right foot forward so it is parallel to your left one. You are teaching me to waltz. The room becomes the dance floor of the Russian emperor. We rotate around the dance floor in a counterclockwise motion among the other imaginary dancers. You tell me that when I am tall enough, you will put one of your hands on my shoulder blade, then it will be easier for me to lead." I like to be led by you. I don't want the music to stop.

I really like this one. You are sitting at the table in the kitchen. I am standing next to you. It is summer. You have a light green T-shirt on and have a knife and a fork in your hands. A big yellow pear is on the plate in front of you. You show me how to peel the pear with the knife and the fork without ever touching it with your hands. I am six years old. I watch you do the magic as the pear peel cleanly separates from the juicy internal flesh. I am impressed. You tell me that you learned it when you were in the Navy. You explain about the table manners and eating etiquette, about making polite conversations and never reaching across the table. I sit at the table facing you. I am careful not to put my elbows on the table.

But this one is my favourite. We are walking next to one another in a forest somewhere in the North of Iran. It is summer. We are lost. You look at the sky and try to find a way out by the position of the sun. You are talking to me, explaining how the sun moves in the sky and how we can use the sun to find an approximate true north. I am seven years old. I hold my head up to look at the sun through the dense leaves of the tall trees. I ask what happens if we cannot find our way out. You make sure that we will. I ask about the wild animals. "What if a leopard attacks us?" You tap the dagger fastened to your belt. You say that you would fight the leopard and won't let it come near me. I know you would. I have no worries in my heart. I wait for you to finish your sky search and sun investigation. Then I see your hand stretch out towards me. I take your hand and feel your strength wrapping me up in a safe embrace. The grasp is firm and secure.

Look! Here it is! This is the birthday card I am getting for you.

Eighteen

"38, 40, 42, …"

The English teacher was walking in the quiet street, peering at house numbers and reading them aloud to herself to find the address. It was a beautiful spring day and the street, which was shaded by tall, lush plane trees, looked extremely peaceful. It was Ava's father's birthday, and the teacher was taking Ava's gift to him. She was happy that she had a chance to go to Ava's parents. It was like meeting part of Ava, after all. Unlike what Ava thought, the teacher was not much occupied those days and did not feel inconvenienced by the visit. She had cancelled a few of her classes and was free for the evening. She loved Ava and was looking forward to doing her a favour.

The first time the English teacher had met Ava was four years ago. She was Ava's English teacher in an esteemed language institute. After having a few classes together, they became close friends. Ava participated in all class discussions and shared her ideas and experiences with her classmates. She frequently volunteered to answer the teacher's questions and give short lectures on various topics in front of the class. She was voluble, unabashed, and exuberant, and the teacher cherished her presence in class. When Ava asked the English teacher for private classes, she immediately accepted, and ever since they met each other almost every week. Mostly, Ava went to the teacher's house and stayed there for a longer time if the teacher did not have any student after her. They talked about a wide range of subject matters. Soon they knew each other's ideas, feelings, and sentiments in most situations without having to talk about them, and both could predict each other's behaviour to a reliable degree of precision.

When Ava left the country, their communication suddenly ended. The teacher felt a loss in her life that she believed could never be filled again. But she also understood why Ava did not, or could not, call her. After the teacher received Ava's letter, she also responded in writing, and a new form of communication was created between them. Writing letters became a habit for both of them, and the teacher received a long letter from Ava almost every other week. Ava's letters were compelling, full of witty remarks, beautiful reminders, and thankful comments, decorated with smiley faces and cartoons. They meant a lot to her.

"44, 46, 48 ..."

48 was the house number. The English teacher looked at the doorbell names and pushed the button. It had an old-fashioned "Ding-Dong" sound that made the teacher smile. Ava's mother opened the door and invited her in. She was expecting her. The teacher had called her a week before, told her about Ava's surprise present, and asked about the right time to drop by. Ava's mother was amazed. She surely did not expect Ava to send or even remember the father's birthday. She had baked some special sweets and had put some music on. When the teacher entered the apartment, Ava's mother welcomed her with a big bright smile, which she fully repaid

with her own. She was also greeted by the delicious smell of the sweets and the energy of George Michael's 'Wake Me Up Before You Go-Go.'

The English teacher smiled. Apparently, Ava's mother had kept her cassettes. She looked around. The apartment was very small, more like a studio. There was only a living room with the kitchen on one side of it and a bedroom and a bathroom on the other side. There was a framed painting of black and white horses above the television. And the teacher remembered that Ava had talked about that painting to answer one of her IELTS questions. The father was sitting on a two-seater sofa in the living room. There was a glass of vodka and an open book on the table in front of him. Déjà vu!

The teacher sat on one of the couches, and Ava's mother brought a glass of orange juice for her. Ava's parents were immensely changed since the last time the teacher had seen them. They had become aged and more grey-haired. Ava's father had particularly changed from an angry man to one whose expression was tired and forlorn. They did not talk much. After a few minutes of formalities, the English teacher reached for her bag and gave Ava's gift to the father, "This is from Ava for your birthday. Happy Birthday!" The gift was wrapped in a simple black wrapping paper with tiny snowflakes sketched on it, and a small envelope was attached to it. On the envelope, Ava had written "*May the Eighth*" with beautiful calligraphy.

The father was entranced. He held the gift in his hands for a long time when the English teacher handed it to him. Ava had told the English teacher that she had never given a gift to his father on his birthday; well, at least not for the past ten years or so. The father had received some drawings and stickers when Ava was a young child, but it was years since he had received a present for his birthday.

The father slowly took the envelope away and started to unwrap the gift. It was Ralph Lauren Polo. The father opened the box and looked at the green cologne for a minute and then sprayed some on his neck. Immediately, a delicious smell permeated the air. The father had already had a smile on his face when he picked up the envelope. He opened it, pulled out the card, and carefully unfolded it.

From where the English teacher was sitting, she could see the drawing of a little girl with long black hair holding a man's hand on the card while the father was reading the inside. The drawing was in black and white, and although both figures on the card – the girl and the man – had indistinct features, the firm hand grip was portrayed clearly with thorough details. The father's hand was slightly shaking holding the card. The teacher looked at him and saw that his eyes were filled with tears. It was a curious situation where the teacher did not know what to do. Tears were so unbecoming to the father's character.

"She's written …" The father falters, looked back at the teacher, stretched his hand, and showed her the inside of the card. Below the typed "Wish You a Happy Birthday," only four words were written with Ava's handwriting.

You are my man!